SPECIAL SAMMY

Special Sammy

Karin Craft

I dedicate this book to all 4 of my children. They are each a wondrous gift to me. I love you all!

Three eggs in a nest
Mama keeping them warm,
What her chicks need best,
Until she lept in alarm!

"Oh, they're moving!" she cried!
She watched the eggs,
Cracks running down the side
A beak came out, then legs...

        Soon, the other two
        Followed their brother.
        A little girl, eyes anew,
        Then a little boy, was the other.

To each, as they came forth
Mama sang to them
"You are special, full of worth
Wondrous gift to me!"

Spencer, the oldest, was strong
He was the first to try.
Slyvie, next, could sing a song
So pretty, listeners would cry.

Sammy, the youngest, was caring
He was small and shy.
Slow to speak, never daring
Quiet, he was passed by.

Sammy had one little wing,
That he was born with,
On its side dangling.
Flying, for him, a myth.

Mama gathered him in
Whispering in his ear
"With you, so special, I win
Wondrous gift to me!"

The first day of school
Sammy and Mama strolled.
But, Spencer and Sylvie,
Flew together, both bold.

Many friends Spencer met
Each challenge, he impressed.
He won every bet
Because he was the best!

Sylvie awed and amazed,
New friends, all those around.
Everyone, they all praised,
Sylvie's glorious sound.

Sylvie, Spencer, wanted known
To Sammy, each saying,
"You are special, our very own
Wondrous gift to us!"

BRAVO!

YAY!

YAY

Each day, Spencer, Sylvie
Were learning and growing,
Having fun, happy,
And it was showing!

But, Sammy had it rough.
Knowing each letter,
All subjects so tough
Frustrated, hoping to be better.

                              As the year went on,
                              Sammy hopped along,
                              With Mama at dawn,
                              Mama singing her song.

"Sammy, my dear
I love you to the sun
So special, never fear
Wondrous gift to me!"

At recess, each day,
Children played games
Sammy could not play.
He could not be the same!

They flew up in the sky
Playing catch, tossing balls.
Sammy, with a sigh,
Wished his wing wasn't small.

                              A girl, Rose, in class
                              Would be mean to him.
                              In the hall, as she'd pass
                              Cry, "Why so dim?"

The teacher said to Rose
One day, "Our Sammy
So special, he knows
He's a wondrous gift to us!"

This great first year,
Coming to an end.
Summer dawning near,
Just around the bend.

Sammy's classmates
All could find numbers
Recite letters, dates,
But Sammy blundered.

He could not proclaim
Which was number one,
Or letters in his name,
When the last day done.

In shame, Sammy thought
To himself that day
"Am I special? I am not
A wondrous gift to anyone!"

Going home that last day
Sylvie and Spencer flying
Sammy, going his way,
Sad, sniffling, crying.

Rose saw him from up high
She teased and taunted him,
"Sammy why do you try?"
But did not see the limb.

Rose hit her head and fell.
In pain, she cried aloud.
Sammy quickly could tell
Flying was not allowed.

He said, "The way, I'll show.
But, first, I'll help you up.
You are special, you know,
Wondrous gift to me!"

Rose, trying not to yelp,
In pain, wondering why,
Sammy chose to help,
When he could've walked by!

Sammy told her jokes,
Games he liked to play,
Toys treasured or maybe broke,
All while, showing her the way.

                          Rose never hopped home.
                          She never saw the flowers,
                          The leaves or soft loam,
                          Or how the trees tower.

At her door, to Sammy
She said, "Thank you, friend,
So special, so uncanny
A wondrous gift to me!"

About the Author:

Karin Craft grew up with a brother with special needs and was diagnosed with a learning disability as a child. She is currently a special education teacher. She lives with her 3 youngest children, husband and 3 cats.

Milton Keynes UK
Ingram Content Group UK Ltd.
UKHW051608250824
447237UK00017B/6